Stone Soup

Other titles illustrated by Tony Ross
available in Picture Lions:

I Want To Be
I Want My Potty
Super Dooper Jezebel
The Knight Who Was Afraid of the Dark
Reckless Ruby
Jenna and the Troublemaker
Carrot Tops and Cottontails

First published in Great Britain by Andersen Press Ltd in 1987
First published in Picture Lions in 1995
10 9 8 7 6
Picture Lions is an imprint of the Children's Division,
part of HarperCollins Publishers Ltd, 77-85 Fulham Palace Road,
Hammersmith, London W6 8JB
Copyright © Tony Ross 1987
The author/illustrator asserts the moral right to be identified
as the author/illustrator of this work.
ISBN: 0 00 664568-2
Printed and bound in Hong Kong

St ne Soup

TONY ROSS

PictureLions

An Imprint of HarperCollins*Publishers*

One day, out walking, the Bad, Bad Wolf came across Mother Hen, pegging out her washing.

He studied the things hanging on the line and he had to admit that they looked of the finest quality.

"Hmmm," thought the Wolf, "there are goodies to be had here."

So he stopped for a chat.

"Good day!" said the Wolf. "I think I shall eat you and then steal all your goodies."

"Thank you very much," squawked Mother Hen. "But before that, perhaps you'd like some soup?"

"That's very kind of you," smiled the Bad, Bad Wolf. "I'd like some soup, *then* I'll eat you."

Mother Hen picked up a stone from
the path.

"I'll make STONE SOUP," she said.
"It's very special."

"It must be," said the Wolf. "I've eaten
soup in all the best places and I've never
heard of it."

Mother Hen boiled some water and
dropped the stone into the pan.

As the Wolf didn't believe that soup could be made from a stone, he sipped a little from a spoon.

"*Peeeew*!" he spat. "It just tastes of hot water."

"Of *course* it does," snapped Mother Hen. "It just needs salt and pepper to bring out the flavour of the stone. While I'm doing that, why don't you just wash a few dishes?"

"Right!" laughed the Bad, Bad Wolf.

When the Wolf had finished the dishes, he tasted the soup again.

"*Yeeeuuugh!*" he howled. "It's *worse*! It's like hot *salty* water now!"

"Maybe a couple of carrots will help the stone to cook," said Mother Hen. "While you're waiting, perhaps you could clean and dust the house?"

"Right!" grinned the Bad, Bad Wolf.

The Wolf tasted the stone soup again.

"It's not much better," he said.

"*Potatoes*!" cried Mother Hen. "Bless us, I did forget the potatoes." And she went to dig some up.

"While you're waiting," she called to the Wolf, "you *could* bring in the washing before it rains."

"Right," said the Bad, Bad Wolf.

Mother Hen let the Wolf taste the soup
again.

"It's better," he said.

"But not quite right," fussed Mother Hen.
"While I get some turnips, could you just
cut that into a few logs?" As she handed
him a tiny axe, she pointed to a huge tree.
"And when you've finished, the stone soup
should be just about ready."

"Right," muttered the Bad, Bad Wolf.

When the tree was cut into logs, the Wolf
tasted the soup yet again.

"It's fine," he said. "Let's eat it *now*."

Mother Hen took a sip.

"Not yet," she said. "A sprout or two will
really complement the flavour of the stone.
While you're waiting, be a sweetie and fix
the TV aerial on the roof."

"Right," groaned the Bad, Bad Wolf.

"The soup smells delicious!" panted the Wolf, when he came down off the roof.

"Ahhh," sniffed Mother Hen, "there's something missing…er…*mushrooms*, that's what it is, *mushrooms*!"

The Wolf stared.

"While you're waiting for the mushrooms to cook in," smiled Mother Hen, "you'd just have time to sweep the chimney."

"Right," snarled the Bad, Bad Wolf.

By the time the Wolf had finished the
chimney, Mother Hen had thrown some
beans, a little cabbage, a few lentils and
a marrow into the pan. Proudly she gave
the Wolf a taste.

He was delighted.

"Who'd have thought," he sighed,
"that a simple *stone* would make such a
glorious soup!"

"I'm glad you liked it," said Mother Hen, when the Wolf had finished the soup. "You can eat me now."

"I *can't*!" gasped the Wolf. "I'm too full."

"Fancy that," said Mother Hen. "You'd better steal my goodies then and be off with you."

The Bad, Bad Wolf leaped to his feet and with a terrible roar...

...he snatched the stone, and took to his heels.